This book belongs to

Language consultant: Betty Root

This is a Parragon Publishing book
This edition published in 2006

Parragon Publishing
Queen Street House
4 Queen Street
Bath, BA1 1HE, UK

ISBN 1-40545-332-X
Printed in China

The Little Ballerinas

Written by Jillian Harker
Illustrated by Claire Henley

From the moment Emily watched her first ballet, she knew what she wanted to be.

The ballet was ***Sleeping Beauty***. Emily loved the beautiful costumes, the wonderful music, and the pretty colored lights. But, most of all, she loved the Prima Ballerina.

Emily couldn't take her eyes off Isabella Ponti as she pirouetted around the stage.

"If only I could dance like that," Emily thought to herself.

Emily was telling her best friend Hannah all about the ballet next day, when her mom came into the bedroom.

"I've got a surprise for you, Emily," said Mom. "I've arranged for you to take some ballet lessons."

Emily jumped up and down on her bed with excitement.

"Wow!" said Hannah. "You're so lucky!"

"It would be perfect if you could come too," said Emily, hugging her friend. "Let's ask your mom."

Hannah's mom agreed, and their first lesson was arranged for the following week. On Saturday, the two girls went out to buy their ballet outfits.

As soon as Emily put on her shoes, she started to do little jumps in the air.

"These are sautés," smiled Emily.

When she slipped into the pretty pink outfit, she felt like a princess. Round and round the shop Emily twirled.

"Watch me do a pirouette!" she called to Hannah and her mom.

"How do you know all these things?" asked Hannah.

"I've been reading about them," replied Emily, "and I can remember exactly how the Prima Ballerina did them."

The girls started their ballet classes the following week. While Hannah worried about each new move, Emily was the quickest to do everything in class.

Whenever their teacher showed them a new step, Emily could do it right away. She could perform a perfect plié...

hold fifth position...

and do a beautiful glissé.

Hannah tried really hard, but she found all the new steps so difficult.

One day, Emily and Hannah arrived at their lesson to find everyone already dancing.

"We're not late, are we?" asked Emily.

"Haven't you heard?" said an older girl. "Isabella Ponti is coming to visit. Isn't it fantastic?"

"No wonder everyone's practicing so hard," said Emily, grabbing her friend's hand. "Come on, Hannah!"

When Isabella Ponti arrived, the excitement grew. The Prima Ballerina explained that she was looking for two girls to dance with her in a performance.

She showed the class the steps she wanted them to practice. Everyone gasped when Isabella danced a beautiful arabesque. None of them had ever tried a pose like that.

Isabella asked the girls to choose partners. “I’ll be back in a few weeks to choose one pair of girls to dance with me,” she told them.

Lots of girls chose Emily as their partner, but no one wanted to dance with Hannah.

Emily thanked the others. "Hannah's going to be my partner," she explained. "She's my best friend."

“Are you sure?” whispered one of the girls.

“I wouldn’t want to dance with anyone else,” replied Emily.

Later, in the park, Emily and Hannah talked about Isabella Ponti's visit.

"I'm nowhere near as good a dancer as you," said Hannah. "You won't be chosen with me as a partner, and you deserve to be. You see, I feel so dizzy when I try to pirouette."

"Are you dizzy right now?" asked Emily, as the pair spun around on the merry-go-round.

"Not really," replied Hannah, puzzled.

"Well, you're going round and round," Emily told her. And she made Hannah dance a pirouette right there.

"But I wobble if I try to balance," insisted Hannah.

"Follow me!" yelled Emily, running along the park wall.

"You see!" said Emily. "You can balance when you don't think about it." And she made her friend do an arabesque right there.

"The most important thing to remember is that dancing is fun," Emily said to her friend.

By the end of that week, Hannah started to believe what Emily had told her.

The two friends practiced together every day, and Emily made sure they shared lots of laughs.

On the day of the Prima Ballerina's visit, each pair showed her what they could do. At last it was Emily's and Hannah's turn to dance.

When Emily smiled at her, Hannah thought of all the fun they'd had ... and she smiled back. She gave the biggest smile of all when they danced an arabesque together.

Isabella Ponti congratulated all the girls on their hard work.

"You all performed really well," she said, "so you haven't made my choice easy. But one pair of dancers stands out—they work together, they smile at each other, and they made me feel that they find dancing fun. I'm choosing Emily and Hannah."

Four weeks later, the night of the performance had finally arrived. As the two friends waited to go on stage, Isabella came out of her dressing room.

"I have something for each of you," she said, holding out two beautiful silver bracelets. Three pairs of ballet shoes dangled from each bracelet. "I hope this will remind you always of our special evening together."

"Oh, thank you!" gasped Emily.

"My bracelet will also remind me that you can do anything with the help of a true friend," added Hannah.

"I agree!" said Emily, smiling. "Now, are you ready? We're on!"

The two girls danced onto the stage after the Prima Ballerina. They performed their steps in perfect time.

As Emily and Hannah jumped and twirled, their two bracelets glittered under the dazzling stage lights.

That evening, it wasn't only the girls' bracelets that sparkled. Just as bright were the smiles the little ballerinas gave each other as they danced—the smiles of true friends.